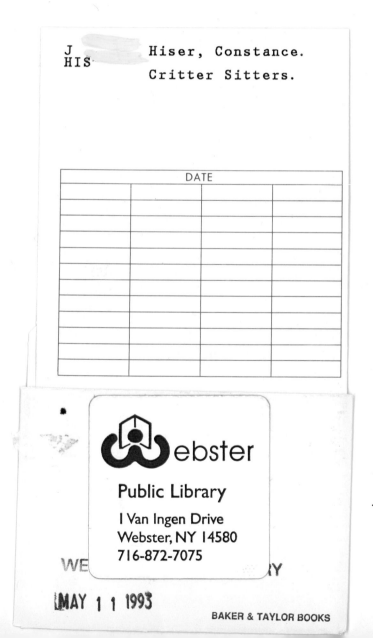

CRITTER SITTERS

Also by Constance Hiser

NO BEAN SPROUTS, PLEASE!
drawings by Carolyn Ewing

GHOSTS IN FOURTH GRADE
drawings by Cat Bowman Smith

DOG ON THIRD BASE
drawings by Carolyn Ewing

CRITTER SITTERS

by Constance Hiser

drawings by Cat Bowman Smith

Holiday House / New York

Library of Congress Cataloging-in-Publication Data
Hiser, Constance.
Critter Sitters / by Constance Hiser : drawings by Cat Bowman
Smith. — 1st ed.
p.   cm.
Summary: James and his friends start a summer pet-sitting business
and are dismayed when their hard-earned cash starts to disappear
from the money box.
ISBN 0-8234-0928-7
[1. Pet sitting—Fiction.   2. Moneymaking projects—Fiction.
3. Mystery and detective stories.]   I. Smith, Cat Bowman, ill.
II. Title.
PZ7.H618Cr   1992   91-23002   CIP   AC
[Fic]—dc20

Contents

CRITTER SITTERS

CHAPTER ONE

Just What We Need!

"Wow, look at this!" T.J. grinned excitedly as she pulled the jacket from its rack at Price's Department Store. "Isn't this terrific?" Her smile got even bigger as she stroked the shiny red satin.

"That's the neatest jacket I ever saw," James agreed, fingering the white cuffs and collar. "Hey, you know what, guys? This is just what we need—we all should have matching jackets, just like this."

"I see what you mean." Norman crowded in for a closer look. "If we all dressed alike, it

1

would sort of be like we were an official gang or club or something. It would be great!"

"I can just see myself in one of these," Mike said, pulling a matching jacket from the rack. He tried it on and smiled at his reflection in the mirror. "We'd be the best-looking gang in school next fall."

"There's just one problem," Pete said gloomily. "Look at the price tag. Where are we going to come up with that kind of money?"

They looked where he was pointing, and everyone gasped. Forty dollars!

"I didn't know a jacket could cost that much," T.J. said.

"Well, so much for that idea," Norman sighed. "That's more than I make in allowance for months and months. Darn it, and we would have looked terrific, too!"

"Hey," Pete suggested hopefully, "you don't suppose our folks would just give us the money, do you?"

James shook his head. "My mom had to get our leaky roof fixed last week. She says

we won't have any extra money for a while. If I want a new jacket, I'll have to get it on my own."

"Me, too," Mike agreed. "My folks already told me they weren't going to buy me a new jacket this year, because my old one still fits."

James thought hard. "Don't give up just yet," he said. "There may be a way for us to get those jackets."

They all stared at him.

"You're crazy, James!" Mike argued. "There's no way we could buy jackets like these."

"Didn't you ever hear of *jobs*?" James asked patiently. "We could earn the money, you know."

Norman made a face. "A *job*?" he repeated. "Who wants to *work* all summer?"

"Besides," T.J. added, flipping one braid over her shoulder, "what kind of jobs are we supposed to get, James? You think we could all go down to the bank and see if they'd hire us as guards? Or maybe we could work on

4

that construction crew that's repaving Second Street. Or Mr. Patelli down at the Ice Cream Shoppe might just—"

"Yeah!" Pete chimed in. "Who's going to hire a bunch of kids?"

"Okay, okay, so I didn't mean a *real* job," James backed down. "But there must be *something* we can do to earn a little money."

"Oh, yeah?" Norman said doubtfully. "Like what?"

"Like washing people's cars," James answered. "Or paper routes, or—oh, I don't know. Lots of things. We just have to find one we can all agree on. And if we work hard and save everything we make, I bet we can get those jackets."

"If they aren't all sold first," Mike sighed, rubbing the sleeve of the jacket he was wearing.

"Those jackets?" They all jumped a little as they looked up to see a saleswoman standing a couple of feet away, smiling at them. "Don't worry, kids, we carry a lot of those—they're very popular. And if we do run out,

5

we can order more of them just for you." She winked. "Why, for just a little extra, we can even have your names put on the back!"

Their eyes got big as they imagined themselves in the shiny jackets with their names across the back.

"I want red," T.J. said dreamily. "With my name in big white letters."

"Blue would be nice, too," Pete pointed out. "Then we could have our names in red."

"We can talk about that later," James said. "Right now the important thing is coming up with the money to buy them. So let's go home and work on it. I bet we can come up with a great idea before lunch."

Norman sighed. "Okay, I'm with you," he said. "Let's just not make it real *work* work, okay?"

Hanging the jackets carefully back on the rack, the gang clattered downstairs, through the perfume department, out the revolving door, and down the sidewalk, hardly noticing the hot summer sun as they hurried to James's house.

*   *   *

"I still vote we get paper routes," Mike said stubbornly, dangling his feet off the edge of James's back porch. "There just aren't that many people to wash cars for—and besides, where would we do it? You have to have a big parking lot or someplace like that, and hoses, and soap, and—"

"Forget the paper route, too," Pete sighed. "Think how early we'd have to get up. My folks would never let me go out alone at four in the morning."

"Hey, I've got it!" James said excitedly. "My mom and I are going to be baby-sitting for my three-year-old cousin Ethan this summer, while my aunt and uncle are out of town. Why couldn't we advertise and get a lot more kids to baby-sit for?"

"That might not be so bad," T.J. said. "I like little kids—as long as they don't need their diapers changed."

"Wouldn't work." Norman shook his head. "The junior high school has a baby-sitting service where all the junior high kids sign

7

up to work—my big sister's on the list. Most of the parents call there. Why would they want a bunch of fourth graders when they could get someone from junior high?"

"Oh, yeah," T.J. sighed. "I forgot about that." She propped her chin on her hands and slumped down. "So what *can* we do? We've just *got* to get those jackets."

"Not now, Tag!" James said irritably, as his fuzzy-faced brown-and-white dog licked his face. "Can't you see we're trying to think?" Suddenly he sat up very straight. "Wait a minute! Tag just gave me a great idea—we can be baby-sitters after all!"

"What?" Norman groaned. "Weren't you listening? We just said that the junior high school—"

"Yeah, yeah, I know," James interrupted. "But the junior high doesn't have a baby-sitting service for *pets*, does it?"

They all looked at him.

"What in the world do you mean, James?" Pete asked.

"Pets!" James repeated. "Cats, dogs, ham-

8

Just What We Need!

sters, goldfish, things like that. Instead of baby-sitters, we can be *pet*-sitters!"

"I get it," T.J. grinned. "Sure, why not? There must be a million people going on vacation right now—people who have pets."

"People who need someone to take care of their pets while they're away," Norman added. "That might not be such a bad idea!"

"Sure!" The more James thought about it, the more enthusiastic he got. "We could keep all the pets in the garage, if we keep the place clean. You can all come over every morning to help feed the animals, and clean their cages, and take the dogs for walks. We could have the money for our jackets in no time."

"We can tell everyone to bring the food and cages for their pets," T.J. suggested. "That way we won't be out a cent, and we could just sit back and watch the money pour in."

"I like that!" Mike grinned. "How do we get started?"

"We can advertise," Norman said. "I've got

9

a bunch of construction paper left from school. We could make lots of posters and put them all over town. Once people hear about our pet-sitting service, we'll have more business than we can handle."

"Great!" Pete jumped up from the porch steps. "I've got lots of art supplies—markers and paste and all that stuff. Why don't we go work at my house?"

"That's terrific, Pete!" T.J. cheered. "I even have a great name for our pet-sitting company. How about this?" She paused, then announced in a loud voice, "Critter Sitters, Incorporated! How do you like it?"

James laughed. "Critter Sitters!" he repeated. "I *do* like that! It's really got a ring to it!"

And the others agreed.

"Let's get started with those posters," Pete said. "We'll make enough to cover this whole town!"

CHAPTER TWO

Paste and Markers

"I wish my mom hadn't already left to pick up my little cousin," James said, reaching for a piece of orange construction paper. "I wanted to make sure everything was okay with her before we went to the trouble of making a million posters."

"Don't worry, she'll say yes," T.J. encouraged him, squinting to see if the lettering was even on her poster. "I wish I were as good at art as you are, Pete. All your posters look terrific. And it was a great idea to use

11

these pictures of animals from your mom's old magazines."

Mike held up one of his posters, yellow construction paper with a cutout of a turtle pasted carefully in one corner, and a ferocious-looking grizzly bear in the other.

"I don't think we ought to try taking care of any *bears,* Mike," Norman said.

"Well, I think it looks good," Mike answered stubbornly. "It's not like anyone in town really *has* a bear, or anything."

"I like it, too," James agreed, tilting his head to one side to study Mike's poster. "Once my mom sees these, she'll *have* to say yes."

"You know what would make it even better?" Norman suggested. "You could write some kind of motto underneath. Critter Sitters, Incorporated—No Pet Too Big, No Pet Too Small."

"Great!" Mike exclaimed, grabbing his marker. "Thanks, Norman!"

"We can't take forever, guys," James

warned. "If Mom says it's okay, we should put all these posters up before supper, if we can."

"That's right," T.J. agreed. "The sooner we hang them, the sooner we'll get our first customers."

Pete's room was very quiet as they all got back to work on their posters—stacks of them.

They were going to make so much money, they wouldn't know what to do with it all!

"Hey, babies! Where are *you* going?" The nasty voice trailed up the sidewalk after them, and they all felt a shiver run up their backbones.

"That Mean Mitchell," T.J. sighed. "He gets worse every day. Why can't he just leave us alone?"

"I *said,* what are you babies doing out here all alone?" Mean Mitchell had caught up to them and pushed past them, and now he stood right in their path. His big yellow dog,

Tiger, was with him, his sharp white teeth bared in a menacing snarl. With a little whimper, Tag pushed closer to James's legs. "Should you little kids be out this close to dark? Aren't you afraid something will get you? Better get home to your mommies!"

James shuffled his feet. "Come on, Mitchell, give us a break. We're not bugging you."

"Oh, yeah?" Mean Mitchell grinned. "Why don't you let *me* decide that? What have you got there? Let me see!" Reaching out one big hand, he yanked the pile of posters from under James's arm.

Mean Mitchell's eyes got narrow as he read the top two or three posters. Uneasily, the kids watched as he shuffled through the stack. Would he rip the posters up, or maybe throw them down on the sidewalk and tramp all over them? After all their work, too.

Mean Mitchell looked at the last poster and smirked, then he shoved the brightly colored stack back at James. "Here," he said.

15

"You kids sure come up with dumb ideas. Out of my way—I have better things to do than play with you babies!"

Pushing James roughly out of the way, Mean Mitchell plodded off down the sidewalk in the opposite direction, with his growling dog trailing at his heels.

"What do you suppose *that* was all about?" T.J. asked, when the bully was out of sight. "I thought he'd tear up our posters for sure!"

"Yeah," Norman agreed. "That's the first time I've ever seen Mean Mitchell decide *not* to do something mean when he had the chance."

"I don't like it, guys," Pete said uneasily. "There's always trouble when Mean Mitchell's around."

"Well?" T.J. demanded, practically dancing up and down on tiptoe as James came out his back door. "What did she say? Is your mom going to let us have our pet-sitting service?"

James grinned and gave them a

16

thumbs-up signal, and the whole gang gave a wild cheer.

"There are a couple of catches, though," he warned them. "Mom says we have to promise to keep the garage clean, and we have to feed and walk the pets all by ourselves. She says we can tell the customers she'll be here, though, just in case anything goes wrong."

"That's no problem," Norman said. "Of course we should do the work, if we get all the money. Is that all?"

"Well . . ." James squirmed a little. "There's just one other thing. I had to promise Mom that we'd help her take care of my little cousin Ethan."

"What?" Mike groaned. "How can we do that and take care of the animals, too?"

"We won't need to watch him all the time," James said quickly. "Just while she's doing her housework and stuff like that. Besides, Ethan's kind of special. He's super-smart—my aunt and uncle have even hired a special teacher for him. I'm sure he'll be easy to take care of." James looked at his friends' frowning faces. "Come on, guys," he continued, "it won't be that bad."

"I don't know—" Pete began.

Just then James's little cousin burst through the back door, wearing a feather headdress and yelling a loud Indian war whoop. "Gotcha!" he screamed, wrapping both legs around Mike's leg and whacking his shins with a plastic tomahawk.

"Ouch!" Mike yelled, trying to pry Ethan loose. "I guess we don't have much choice, but I have to tell you, I don't think I like this."

"It'll be okay," James promised. "We'll all work together. You'll see."

"Oh, I almost forgot." T.J. reached into her shirt pocket, while Ethan did an Indian dance around her. "Look what I found to put our money in." She pulled out a small tin box.

Norman groaned. "Teddy bears?" he said. "Did you have to bring a box with teddy bears all over it, T.J.?"

"Don't you make fun of my box!" T.J. snapped. "My folks gave it to me last Valentine's Day, full of candy. Besides, I didn't notice that *you* remembered to bring anything to put our money in!"

"It's a great box," James said hastily, before Norman could answer. "Thanks. Now what do you say we all get busy putting posters up? We've got an awful lot of them to take care of before dark. No, Ethan, you have to stay here with Mom. I'll play with you after supper."

With James's little cousin whining at them from the kitchen door, they headed for the street, posters under their arms. It was already a lot of hard work, getting rich!

CHAPTER THREE

Opera Is for the Birds

"It's about time you got here!" James greeted his friends when they pounded on the door early the next morning. "You'll never guess who called last night and wants us to pet-sit!"

"Santa Claus," T.J. guessed, yawning sleepily.

"The president of the United States," Mike suggested, looking grouchy.

"The Man in the Moon," Norman said, stretching.

"Oh, come on, guys," James interrupted,

before Pete could guess, "this is big news. We might have our jackets a lot sooner than we thought."

"Really?" T.J. asked. "What are you talking about, James?"

"You'll never believe it," James said again. He paused to give them time to wonder about it. Then he announced in a triumphant voice, *"Mrs. Adamson-Smythe!"*

They gasped. *"The* Mrs. Adamson-Smythe?" Pete said. "The rich lady who lives in the huge old house up on the hill?"

"That's the one," James answered, enjoying their amazement. "She's in my mom's exercise class, and she saw one of the posters that Mom took to class with her last night. Anyway, Mrs. Adamson-Smythe is going to be out of town for two weeks, and the place where she usually boards her pet is closed for two weeks for remodeling. She and Mom got to talking. She wasn't sure we were old enough to take care of her pet, but when she heard Mom was going to help us, she said she'd think about it. Then she called

21

late last night and I talked to her. And after I promised we'd take good care of Amazon—"

"Wait a minute," T.J. interrupted. *"Amazon?* What kind of name is *that* for a dog?"

"Who said it was a dog?" James grinned. "And before you guess again, it's not a cat either."

"Don't tell me it's a crocodile or a snake or something like that!" Pete moaned. "If you do, I'm out of here."

"Nothing that bad," James laughed. "Amazon is her parrot—her *talking* parrot. She says he's a very valuable bird—he even sings! That's why she was worried about leaving him with us. But thanks to my mom, she decided to give us a chance."

"I'm not sure it's such a great idea, James." Norman sounded worried. "What do we know about taking care of a parrot?"

"Mrs. Adamson-Smythe is bringing instructions," James promised. "She has special food for him and everything. Don't worry, it'll be a cinch. But here's the very best part." His grin got wider. "If we take

22

good care of Amazon, Mrs. Adamson-Smythe promised to pay us a hundred dollars. That's twenty dollars apiece!"

Their mouths fell open and their eyes got big. A hundred dollars!

"That's not all," James went on. "She has friends who are looking for someone to pet-sit, too—and she said she'd call all of them this morning. Before long, this place is going to look like Noah's ark!"

"Wow!" Mike exclaimed. "Who would have thought we could earn so much money so fast?"

"When's Amazon due to arrive?" Norman asked.

"Right after lunch," James said. "So we'd better get started cleaning out the garage. We have a lot of work to do before the pets get here." He made a face. "Oh, yeah—and we have to take care of my cousin this morning, while Mom weeds the garden."

"Well, that's fair enough," T.J. admitted, but they all looked gloomy. "Oh, great, here he comes now."

James's mother brought Ethan to the kitchen door and scooted him out onto the back porch. He was wearing a long red cape and a black mask, pretending to be a superhero. "You the bad guys. I'm the good guy!" he yelled. "Bam! Pow!"

"Ouch!" James complained, as Ethan's fists crashed into his stomach. "Okay, okay, you got me, Superman—but before I go to jail you have to help us clean out the garage."

"No!" Ethan whined, dancing on Mike's toes.

The kids looked at each other. This was going to be harder than they thought.

After hours of sweeping and dusting and hosing out the garage—not to mention chasing Ethan—the kids were exhausted by the time Mrs. Adamson-Smythe arrived in her big black car. She stood in the middle of the garage with a covered birdcage in her hand, her high-heeled foot tapping the floor as she looked around the clean, sunny room.

"We'll take care of Amazon as if he were our very own parrot," T.J. promised, while Ethan stood on tiptoe, trying to peek into the cage.

"I'm sure you will," Mrs. Adamson-Smythe said, setting the cage on a shelf. She opened her purse and took out several pages of paper with instructions typed on them. "Here's his feeding schedule, and how to give him his medicine, and how to clean his cage properly, and . . ."

The kids glanced at each other. It seemed a lot harder to take care of a parrot than a cat or a dog.

"And you must be sure to talk to Amazon a lot," Mrs. Adamson-Smythe finished, handing the papers to James. "Parrots are very sociable birds—they like a lot of company. If he likes you, maybe he'll even sing for you."

She removed the cloth that had been covering the cage, and they all pushed for a better look at the red-and-green parrot. Then Mrs. Adamson-Smythe made some chirping sounds, and, to the kids' amazement, the bird opened his beak—and a song actually came out, in a voice that sounded as if he were gargling with a mouthful of gravel.

"What's that he's singing?" Norman asked. "I can't understand a word!"

Mrs. Adamson-Smythe smiled. "That's because he's singing in Italian," she explained. "It's an opera composed by Wolfgang Amadeus Mozart—you have studied Mozart in school, haven't you? Amazon and I simply adore opera, don't we, precious?" And she made some kissing sounds.

The kids tried to look enthusiastic. They'd all had to listen to opera at school, when cranky old Miss Feldstein, their music teacher, had played a lot of tapes for them. They hadn't liked opera much then—and the music didn't sound any better with a parrot singing it.

"That's great, Mrs. Adamson-Smythe," Mike said, when the song came to an end at last.

"Well, I have a plane to catch," she said,

pushing her glasses up on her nose and giving Amazon's cage one last pat. "Oh, by the way, I think you can expect a lot more animals soon—a dog, two cats, a parakeet, and three hamsters, to be exact. I told my friends you were responsible and would take excellent care of their pets."

"Thanks, Mrs. Adamson-Smythe," James said, as he opened the garage door for her, "that's really nice of you."

When Mrs. Adamson-Smythe had finally driven off in her big black car, the kids stood in the garage and stared at the parrot, who stared right back at them.

"Opera!" Norman shook his head, looking disgusted. "Yuck!"

"Yuck!" Ethan agreed, trying to climb up James's leg for a better look at Amazon. "I want the birdie, James!"

"Well, you can't have him," James said, pushing him back down. "Isn't it about time you took a nap?"

"No," Ethan declared. "Gimme birdie! Gimme birdie! Gimme birdie, James!"

Pete sighed. "Something tells me this is going to be a long two weeks," he said, pulling Ethan away from the cage just in time to rescue his fingers from Amazon's big, strong beak.

CHAPTER FOUR

The Mummy Walks

"Hey, James!" T.J. shrieked, as James walked into the garage a few days later. "Winston's gotten out of his cage, and Spanky's been chasing him! I'm afraid that dumb lizard is going to get himself eaten alive!"

James groaned. "Winston's out *again*?" he said. "How many times does that make now?"

"Who cares?" T.J. snapped, shoving a large, gray-and-white cat into James's arms. "Here, you hold Spanky while I try to get

Winston. I think he's hiding over there, behind the big toolbox."

The big cat was squirming and twisting frantically in James's arms, desperate to get loose and catch a lizard dinner. One sharp claw raked across James's shoulder, right through his T-shirt.

"Ouch!" James yelled. "Hey, T.J., hurry up, can't you? This cat is scratching me to death, and I still have to change all the cats' litter boxes—unless you want to do it this time."

"Oh, no!" She shook her head as she shoved the big green lizard back into his cage. "I did it yesterday. Besides, it's almost time to feed everything—again."

"Yeah." He nodded. "It seems like it's *always* time to feed everything. Last night I dreamed about cat food. Oh, no!" He slapped his hand to his forehead. "Ethan! I took him to the house to use the bathroom, and when I heard you yelling out here, I forgot and left him in there all by himself!"

31

"Great." T.J. scrambled up from the floor and followed him. "He's probably torn your whole house apart by now, swinging on the curtains and playing Tarzan, like he did yesterday."

Quickly, they ran up the back steps and into the house. "Ethan!" James called. "Ethan, where are you?"

"Wooooooooooooooooo!"

A loud, eerie wailing from the hallway made both kids jump. T.J. shrieked as a strange figure waddled toward them from the direction of the bathroom. Whatever it was was short and chubby and covered with miles and miles of something that looked like—

"Toilet paper!" James yelled, angrily grabbing a handful of the stuff and ripping it away from his cousin's grinning face. "Ethan, what have you been doing with our *toilet paper*?"

"I'm a mummy," Ethan answered, looking delighted with himself. "Wooooooooooooooooo!"

James sighed. "Well, we'd better get you

out of all this stuff," he said. "What a mess! Come on, let's go to your room."

"No," Ethan said stubbornly. "Wooooo-ooooooooo!" he wailed, still waving his arms.

"Ethan," James told him firmly, "if you don't get in there right now, I'm . . . I'm going to put Winston down your pants!"

"What?" Ethan yelped.

James put on his sternest face. "And my mom will say *no pie for you,*" he went on. "She'll mean it, too. You'll have to eat bean sprouts for dessert instead."

"I'll go," Ethan promised, already scrambling for his room.

In Ethan's room, James and T.J. tore off pieces of toilet paper from Ethan's clothes and tossed them into the wastebasket.

"I don't see how anyone could sleep in here with *that* thing on the floor," T.J. said.

"What thing?" James looked where she was pointing. "Oh, you mean the bearskin rug. What's the matter with it?"

"What's the *matter* with it?" T.J. shuddered as she pulled one last shred of toilet paper from Ethan's hair. "It's awful—all those teeth, and those horrible glaring eyes! I don't know why your mom keeps it in the house."

"She doesn't like it much either," James told her. "That's why she keeps it where no one can see it. But she can't get rid of it. My uncle Wesley got it on an expedition to Alaska. An Eskimo hunter gave it to him, and he couldn't turn it down. He didn't want it, so he sent it to Mom. She feels terrible that the bear had to die to make an ugly rug, but she couldn't refuse either."

"I *like* the bear," Ethan said, pouncing on the floor to give the bear a big hug.

"Listen," James said. A loud chorus of barks and snarls announced that the others had returned from walking Skipper, Peanuts, and Roscoe, the dogs. "I'll go out and help. Why don't you stay here, T.J., and play with Ethan?"

"Okay," groaned T.J., as she pushed herself up from the floor to grab Ethan, before he could follow his big cousin out the door.

The next day, all the kids helped to walk the dogs. It was a long walk. The dogs got their leashes tangled nine times, tried to chase four cats, and dragged the kids through three flower beds. By the time they turned the corner onto James's street, they were all hot, tired, out of breath, and cranky—all except the dogs. The dogs were having a wonderful time.

"Oh, no," Mike groaned, as they reached the last block. "It's Mean Mitchell. That's really all we need."

"Maybe we'll get lucky and he'll leave us alone," Norman sighed.

But Mean Mitchell wasn't about to do that. "Hi, babies!" he called, as they came to James's yard. "Poor kiddies, isn't it hot to be working so hard?"

"So what if it's hot?" T.J. snapped. "We're making money."

Mean Mitchell shook his head. "Wise up,"

he sneered. "Some people have lots of money, and they don't have to work for it either."

"What do you mean by that?" James asked uneasily.

Mean Mitchell snickered. "Don't you worry your hot little head about it," he said. "Well, I think I'll be on my way. I have a big banana split waiting at Patelli's Ice Cream Shoppe."

The kids frowned. Since when did Mean Mitchell have money for banana splits?

Then Pete poked James in the ribs, and they all looked where he was pointing. T.J. gasped, and Norman clapped his hand over her mouth so Mean Mitchell wouldn't hear.

Was that a *ten-dollar bill* poking from the top of Mean Mitchell's jeans' pocket? He had never had that kind of money before!

"That's strange," Norman said, as they watched the bully stroll down the street. "James, do you suppose—"

James nodded. "Yeah," he said. "I don't

like the looks of this. Let's get to the garage and check our money box!"

"It's not here," James groaned, as he finished counting their money. "This morning we had thirty-eight dollars and twenty cents. Now we have just twenty-eight dollars and twenty cents—we're missing exactly ten dollars!"

"I knew it," T.J. exclaimed. "The minute I saw that ten-dollar bill in his pocket, I knew he'd taken our money."

"But why just ten dollars?" Mike asked. "Why didn't he take everything?"

"He thought we wouldn't notice a few dollars," Pete guessed. "That does it. We've got to hide our money—someplace no one will ever think to look."

"What about in this toolbox?" Norman asked. "Under all these screwdrivers and pliers and things."

"Good idea." James carefully arranged a layer of tools and nails over the money box,

completely hiding it from sight. "No one could find it now."

"Hey, kids." James's mom stood in the garage door, holding Ethan's hand. Today he was dressed in a huge black cowboy hat, and he was riding a stick horse. "I want you to watch Ethan while I make a phone call. Why, what's the matter? What are you doing with that toolbox?"

James sighed. "It's awful, Mom," he said. "Just awful. A thief has struck Critter Sitters, Incorporated!"

CHAPTER FIVE

Caught Red-Handed!

"Uh-oh," Norman muttered a few afternoons later, as they returned from lunch at T.J.'s house. "Look, Mean Mitchell's hanging around again."

Sure enough, the bully and his big yellow dog were blocking the sidewalk.

"It's a good thing we hid the money," T.J. whispered.

"Hi, babies!" Mean Mitchell greeted them. "Just dropped by to show you my new ball and glove. Aren't they beauties?" He shoved his treasures under their noses. "Not that you have time to play ball, since you're so busy sitting for all those cute little critters."

"Hey," Norman said, "those gloves are expensive! I saw one at the sports shop. Did you come into some money or something?"

"That's none of your business," Mean Mitchell sneered, throwing the ball up into the air and catching it with a *plop* in his new glove. "Let's just say I didn't have to work for it, the way some dummies do."

Now the same horrible thought was on all of their minds.

"Did you find it on the sidewalk?" T.J. asked.

Mean Mitchell glared. "I *said,* that's none of your business! You're about to make me mad."

"But, Mitchell," James began, "we were just wondering—"

"That did it!" Mean Mitchell yelled. "Sic 'em, Tiger!"

With a ferocious growl, Mean Mitchell's drooling dog lunged at them, scattering them across the yard while Mean Mitchell

41

laughed. The kids reached the garage with Tiger at their heels, and didn't stop running until they had slammed the door in his snarling face. Quickly, James locked the door, and they leaned against the wall, panting.

"That was a close one," Pete said.

"Never mind that now," Norman said. "What about our money?"

"You guys keep a lookout for Mean Mitchell," James answered. "I'll get the money box out."

Hastily, he opened the big toolbox. It took only a glimpse to tell him that someone had already been there—the layer of nails and tools had been swept aside, and the lid of the money box was barely pushed down.

"Uh-oh," James muttered, as he emptied the money on the garage floor and began to count.

"Over twenty-five dollars missing," he groaned, five minutes later. "We had sixty-three dollars last night—now we have just thirty-seven dollars and thirteen cents."

"Mean Mitchell strikes again!" T.J. declared, clenching her fists.

"Who else?" Pete sighed. "I bet he came in while we were at T.J.'s house. He must have gone right to the store and come back here to show off."

"What else could possibly go wrong?" Mike sounded as if he were ready to cry.

"Awk!" The parrot's rusty voice cut through their gloom. The bird gave a few harsh squawks and mumbles, then he opened his beak and began his Mozart song—for what seemed like the millionth time that day. Immediately, all the dogs began to yelp, all the cats started to yowl, and Winston the lizard began to scuttle back and forth inside his cage.

"Great," Norman said, "just what we need. An afternoon of opera."

And they held their hands over their ears as Amazon screeched, "Figaro, Figaro, Figaro . . ."

*　　*　　*

"You know, James," Pete said an hour later, when they had finished changing all the litter boxes and feeding Winston and clipping Amazon's toenails, "we ought to take the dogs for their afternoon walk. We're a couple of hours late already."

James looked at his watch. "You're right. But I'd hate to leave right now. I think I saw Mean Mitchell pass the house a few minutes ago. Maybe I should take our money into the house, so Mom can keep an eye on it."

"Wait a minute," Norman said, as James lifted the money box from the toolbox. "I have a better idea—a way to find out for sure who's been taking our money."

"Yeah?" Mike asked. "How?"

"Well, we know Mean Mitchell's probably spying on us," Norman said. "He'll know the minute we leave with the dogs. I bet the second we're out of sight he'll head straight for the garage—and our money."

"We know that already," T.J. said.

"But what if we pretend to take the dogs out, then double back and hide behind those

44

big bushes at the back of the yard?" Norman suggested. "We could see everything from there, and if Mean Mitchell went into the garage, we could nab him red-handed!"

"It might work," James admitted. "We could even make it easier by leaving the money right out here in plain sight on this shelf, where he won't be able to resist grabbing it."

"And *then* what?" T.J. asked. "Don't tell me you're brave enough to try and stop him—even if you saw him with our money right there in his grubby hands. His dog could shred us just like confetti, and you know it."

"But we could use my mom as backup," James explained. "She's inside with Ethan. If Mean Mitchell takes our money, I'll sneak around behind the trash cans and the bushes and get her. He might act brave around us, but he's not so brave around grown-ups. And I'd like to see *anyone* smart off to my mom when she gets good and mad!"

45

"Good idea," said T.J. "Let's do it."

A few minutes later, the entire gang, with Roscoe, Peanuts, and Skipper on leashes, was hidden behind the bushes that ran along the back of James's yard. Norman had thought of everything. He pulled three rawhide chew bones out of his pocket and tossed them to the dogs, who immediately settled down in the grass for a good chew.

"Look," said Mike, a few minutes later, "he didn't waste much time—here he comes now."

Sure enough, Mean Mitchell was ambling around the corner of James's house, headed straight for the garage. Looking cautiously from side to side, he crept across the yard and over to the garage window. Then he cupped his hands around his eyes and pressed his nose against the windowpane.

"At least Tiger's not with him," T.J. whispered. "I bet it's not two minutes before he's in there swiping our money, the big fat crook."

"Shh," James warned, "he's about to go in!"

He was right—Mean Mitchell had eased the garage door open and sneaked inside.

"Why, the dirty rat!" T.J. was beginning to lose her temper. "Who does he think he is, just walking into your garage like that? I'll show him!"

And, before the boys could stop her, she had left her hiding place and marched across the backyard, heading right for the garage. As they watched, she stretched up on tiptoe and pushed her face against the window.

"Oh, great," James sighed, "she had to go and get brave all of a sudden. Come on, we'd better see if we can keep her from getting her neck broken!"

"And spoiling my plan," Norman added.

They paused just long enough to tie the dogs' leashes to the lilac bushes. Then they stooped low and scuttled across the backyard like four giant crabs. It seemed like a million miles to the garage, but at last they

47

were there, clustered around T.J.'s feet.

Norman tugged at her jeans' leg. "Down!" he hissed. "He'll see you!"

T.J. made a face at him. "I'm going to keep an eye on him," she whispered back. "So far he hasn't even looked at the money—he's just standing around looking at all the animals."

Carefully, the boys straightened up. Holding their breaths, they peeked through the window—and there was Mean Mitchell, standing in front of Amazon's cage, staring at the parrot.

"What is he up to?" Norman breathed. "Why doesn't he grab the money?"

Just then, Mean Mitchell stuck out one pudgy finger and poked Amazon's feathery chest. "Awk!" the parrot squawked, and its big curved beak clamped down hard on Mean Mitchell's finger. "Ouch, ouch, ouch!" Mean Mitchell yelped, hopping up and down. "That hurt, you dirty bird!"

"Awk!" Amazon repeated. "Help, murder, police!"

"Why, you . . ." Mean Mitchell snarled.

"Hey, mister."

Mean Mitchell jumped a foot into the air as the small voice greeted him from the garage doorway.

"Oh, no," Norman moaned softly, "it's your cousin. Isn't your mom supposed to be watching him?"

Sure enough, it was Ethan, dressed in his soldier helmet.

"That's the lady's birdie," he informed the bully. "Where's James? Auntie wants him."

"Oh, for pete's sake!" Mean Mitchell exploded. "Outta my way, baby—I don't want to stick around here, after all."

Pushing Ethan out of the way, he stormed outside, still sucking on his bloody finger.

"You're mean, mister!" Ethan shouted after him. "Bang, bang, you're dead!"

"We'd better get out of here," Pete said, but before they had time to move, Mean Mitchell barreled around the corner of the garage and almost knocked Norman and T.J. over.

"What are you doing here?" he demanded, glaring at them.

"It's my backyard," James said, somehow finding his voice. "What are *you* doing here?"

"If I want to go somewhere, I go," Mean Mitchell sneered, "and don't you forget it."

"But what were you doing in James's garage?" T.J. piped up.

"I was just looking at all the puppy dogs and kitty cats and cute little furry things that bite, okay?" Mean Mitchell snorted.

"What did you do to that parrot, Mitchell?" James asked, his heart pounding. "And what about my cousin? If you laid one finger on him, I'll—"

"Oh, who needs this?" Mean Mitchell huffed. "I've got better things to do. Out of my way, you stupid Critter Sitters."

He tramped across the yard, past the bushes and the barking dogs, and disappeared down the alley.

The kids rushed into the garage.

"That was weird," Mike said, as they hurried to make sure the animals were all right. "He didn't steal the money after all. What was he doing here?"

"He'd have taken the money if Ethan hadn't come in when he did," T.J. insisted, bending down to give the little boy a hug.

"And Amazon might have had his neck wrung." James shuddered, just thinking about it. "Lucky Ethan showed up."

"Yep," Ethan said excitedly. "He's the bad guy. Bang! Bang! Can I have a cookie?"

"Ethan, where's my mom?" James said, lifting his cousin off the ground. "You shouldn't be running around by yourself, but I'm glad you were. You saved Amazon's life."

"Let's get him a cookie," Pete suggested, as they headed for the kitchen door.

They agreed that they could all use a few cookies to calm their hammering hearts and shaking knees.

CHAPTER SIX

The Thief Strikes Again

"If that parrot sings that song one more time, I'm going to wring his neck myself," T.J. muttered, as she slid clean paper into the bottom of Amazon's cage. "I've never been so tired of anything in my whole life."

"What are you complaining about?" Mike grumbled, emptying a new bag of kitty litter into one of the cats' litter boxes. "This has got to be the smelliest, messiest, most disgusting job in the world."

"You don't have anything to gripe about," Norman informed them. "The dogs went

53

wacko on their walk today and dragged me down the street."

"Yeah, and it's *hot* out there," Pete added. "I thought I'd melt. You guys were just hanging around here in a cool garage, and—"

"Cool!" T.J. exploded. "I suppose that's why my T-shirt is sopping wet!"

"Hey, stop it, guys!" James hurried to head off an argument. "We've all been working hard, and we're all tired. But won't it be worth it when we get those terrific jackets?"

"Yeah," T.J. agreed. "We have to keep thinking about them. I want red. With my name in big white letters."

"Blue would be nice, too," Pete reminded her, "with our names in red."

"If we ever get our jackets, that is," Norman snapped. "If Mean Mitchell gets any more of our money, it'll never happen."

"I wish we could have caught him in the act," Mike sighed. "Now we'll never be able to prove anything."

"And we'll probably never get our money

back either," Pete said gloomily. "Ethan, did you see anyone take our money?"

James's little cousin, who was running around the garage wearing his pirate hat and eye patch and waving a plastic sword, stopped and shook his head.

"No, Pete," he said, and walked off solemnly.

"It's not all that bad," James reminded them. "Even without the stolen money, we'll have enough for our jackets, once people have paid us everything they owe us. We'll get those jackets—wait and see."

"But I keep thinking of all the fun we gave up this summer," Norman said. "Swimming, riding our bikes, going to the movies—it's a good thing those are such neat jackets, or I'd say we wasted a perfectly good summer."

T.J. stood and stretched. "I'll just be glad when Mrs. Adamson-Smythe comes and gets her parrot tomorrow," she said. "If I hear that 'Figaro' thing one more time, I'm going to start screaming and never stop!"

*   *   *

"Yoo-hoo!" Mrs. Adamson-Smythe waved one gloved hand at them from the garage door. "Here I am to get my darling Amazon. Oh, there you are, precious! Were you a good boy while Mama was gone?"

She rushed toward the parrot's cage, making little kissy noises, while Amazon pretended not to know who she was.

"It seems you took very good care of him," she said, after taking a good look at her parrot. "You've certainly earned your hundred dollars."

The kids gasped as she took a crisp, new hundred-dollar bill from her purse and handed it to James. It was theirs, all theirs!

"We'll carry the cage to your car for you," James offered, sticking the money into his pocket. "Ethan, you stay right here."

"Bye-bye birdie," Ethan said, and he walked back into the garage.

James and Norman carried Amazon's cage out to the driveway, while Pete, Mike, and T.J. tagged along behind.

"I'm going to keep recommending Critter Sitters to my friends," Mrs. Adamson-Smythe promised, getting into her car.

"Thank you, ma'am," James smiled, although he wasn't really sure he wanted to keep on pet-sitting, once they had their jackets. He wasn't sure he even wanted to *see* a cat or dog or hamster again—except for Tag, of course. And he *knew* he didn't want anything to do with any more parrots.

The kids waved as Mrs. Adamson-Smythe drove away, then headed back to the garage.

"That should be all the money we need," T.J. said. "A lot of people picked up their pets today. So even without the money we lost, we can go downtown after supper and get our jackets!"

"Yeah!" Mike agreed enthusiastically. "How long will it take to have our names put on them?"

"Maybe they can do it while we wait," Norman said. "I wonder if— What's the matter, T.J.?"

The Thief Strikes Again

T.J., who had opened up the money box to count their earnings, was sitting on the floor, and her face looked pale.

"James," she said, "I saw you put that hundred-dollar bill into your pocket. What did you do with the rest of the money?"

"Do with it?" James echoed. "I put it in the box and I put the box on the shelf, the way I always do. What's wrong?"

"See for yourself," she said.

They all gulped in disbelief, for there on the floor, the money box stood open—and it was completely empty!

"And look at this!" T.J. cried, pointing to a corner of the garage. "A brand-new baseball—over there on the floor! Where have we seen a new baseball lately?"

"Mean Mitchell!" they all groaned together.

CHAPTER SEVEN

Banana Splits and Bubble Gum

"I knew it! I just knew it!" T.J. exploded. She scooped the baseball up from the floor and waved it in their faces. "This proves everything!"

"Yeah," James agreed. "It looks as if Mean Mitchell's been the thief all along."

"Ethan," Pete asked, "did you see anyone in the garage? Was there anyone near our money?"

Ethan looked up. "I don't know," he said. "I been busy." He pointed his finger at Pete. "Pow! Pow!"

"What do we do now?" Mike asked.

"I guess the first thing is to find Mean Mitchell," James said. "It sounds like he took our money—maybe he's spending it now. But before we go anywhere, I'll take our hundred dollars inside and get Mom to keep her eye on it—and on Ethan, too."

"Let's try downtown," T.J. suggested, when they were all walking along the sidewalk. "That's where the stores are."

They had just turned onto Main Street when they ran into another fourth grader, Nick. He looked excited about something.

"What's up, Nick?" Mike asked.

"It's Mean Mitchell!" Nick exclaimed. "He must have robbed a bank!"

"What are you talking about?" T.J. asked.

"Well, you know Mean Mitchell—he never has any money," Nick explained. "But he just parked a *brand-new bike* at the ice-cream store. And I just saw him eat *three* banana splits, and he had five or six big packages of bubble gum in his pocket. I wonder where he got the money to buy all that stuff?"

"Yeah," Norman said, "I wonder? Come on, guys."

"Look," Pete whispered a few minutes later, as they peered through the window of Patelli's Ice Cream Shoppe. "There he is. And he's still eating."

"With *our* money, yet!" T.J. exclaimed. "I say we go make him give it back."

"Wait a minute, T.J.—" James began. But she had already opened the door and stamped into the ice-cream parlor.

"Mitchell Monaghan!" she yelled. "We want our money back!"

Mean Mitchell got slowly to his feet, his face red and angry, his eyes narrowed to little slits.

"Beat it, brat," he snorted. "I don't know what you're talking about."

"We know you were in James's garage!" T.J. hissed. "We found *this*!"

Triumphantly, she held up the baseball.

"Hey, where did you get that?" Mean

Mitchell demanded. "That's mine!" Snatching the ball, he glared at T.J. angrily.

"Aha!" she said. "So you admit it!"

"I didn't take your dumb ol' money!" Mean Mitchell yelled. "That ball must have fallen out of my pocket. Maybe one of those dogs found it."

"Maybe so, but that doesn't explain where you got all that money you've been spending lately," Pete said, in a shaky voice.

Mean Mitchell glared at them. "It's none of your business," he said. "But since you're making such a big deal out of it, I'll tell you. My dad's uncle died and left me some money in his will. Now you know—so beat it!"

"What a lie!" T.J. shouted. "Who'd believe *that*?"

"Here, here! What's going on?" Mr. Patelli bustled from behind the counter, and he wasn't smiling. "I won't stand for this racket in the shop! What's the trouble?"

"He took our money!"

"I did not!"

Mr. Patelli shook his head. "I can't hear

you if you all yell at once. One at a time!"

"That's *our* money Mitchell's using for those banana splits," T.J. complained. "We found his baseball! We know he was in James's garage!"

"I was not!" Mean Mitchell bellowed. "And I didn't take your money!"

"Did too!"

"Did not!"

Mr. Patelli shushed them. "I can settle this. Mitchell, isn't your dad home now? Give me your phone number, and I'll call and check your story out. If he says the money's yours, the kids will leave you alone. Right?"

Reluctantly, the kids nodded. Mean Mitchell mumbled his phone number, and Mr. Patelli disappeared into the small room behind the ice-cream counter. A few minutes later, he came back, shaking his head.

"Well, kids," he said, "you got the wrong idea this time. Mitchell's dad says his late uncle really did leave him money in his will.

Whether or not he was in James's garage, the money is Mitchell's, all right."

"What?" T.J. gasped. "It can't be true!"

"As a matter of fact," Mr. Patelli said, "your dad wants you to come home now, Mitchell. You have to cut the grass."

Scowling, Mean Mitchell grabbed his baseball cap and tramped out of the store, slamming the door in the confused faces of James and his friends.

"I'm sorry you lost your money, kids," Mr. Patelli said. "Would you feel better if I made you each an ice-cream cone? On the house, of course."

James sighed. "Not much better," he said.

"But we won't say no to free ice cream," Pete added, nodding at the rest of the gang. "Thanks, Mr. Patelli."

The double-scoop ice-cream cones were delicious. But there were some things even ice cream didn't help. Not even pistachio fudge ripple with nuts and a cherry on top.

CHAPTER EIGHT

An Amazing Discovery

"I wonder how that baseball got into my garage," James sighed, as they dragged their feet down the sidewalk. "Maybe Mean Mitchell really did drop it there. We know he's been sneaking in to look at the animals."

"I still have trouble believing he didn't take our money," T.J. grumbled. "I was so sure about it, too."

"I'd like to know where all that cash disappeared to," said Pete. "I mean, we know it didn't just grow wings and fly out of the garage. And we know none of us took it. So—"

67

"Oh, yeah?" Norman butted in. "And exactly how do we know that? Wasn't that a new model car I saw in your room yesterday, Pete? Where did you get the money for it?"

The others gasped, and Pete's mouth fell open.

"What do you mean by *that*?" he demanded. "That model car was a birthday present from my grandmother. For that matter, where did you get the money for the new shirt you wore yesterday?"

"Are you saying I stole it?" Norman growled, turning red in the face.

"Cut it out, guys!" T.J. yelled, while James and Mike pushed between Pete and Norman. "I thought friends were supposed to trust each other!"

Norman stared down at the toes of his sneakers. "You're right," he said. "I don't know why I said that. I'm sorry."

Pete held out his hand. "Me, too," he said. "I guess we're all just hot and tired and worried."

"I'll make a pitcher of cold lemonade," James suggested, as they reached his back porch. "It might make us all feel better."

Wiping their streaming faces, the kids followed James into his kitchen. Then, carrying their drinks, they headed for the living room.

"Shh," James's mother warned, looking up from her magazine, "Ethan's taking a nap, thank goodness."

"Hey, Mom, where's that hundred-dollar bill I asked you to watch?" asked James.

"On the bookshelf, by the potted plant." His mom pointed.

James looked. "It's not here," he said. "Are you sure?"

"That's funny!" She came to look. "I really thought I put it there. Did it fall behind the bookcase?"

But there was nothing behind the bookcase, or under the rug, or between any of the books.

"Don't get upset, kids," James's mother

69

said. "It's got to be here somewhere—it couldn't just walk away."

"Yeah," James sighed, "that's what we've told ourselves all day."

"Maybe I was wrong about putting it on the bookshelf," his mother answered. "Why don't we look in some of the other rooms? And try the fridge. I might have put it in there accidentally when I got a glass of iced tea."

But the money wasn't in the bathroom, or the TV room, or the refrigerator.

"There's just one more room downstairs," James said. "The guest room. And Ethan's asleep in there."

"Go ahead and search," James's mother said. "Just be quiet, and try not to wake him up."

On tiptoe, they moved into the guest room.

Ethan wasn't sleeping on his bed. Instead, he was rolled up in a little ball, right in the middle of the fuzzy white polar bear rug. His red fireman's hat lay beside him, and

James's dog, Tag, lay snoring at his feet.

"Hey, James!" Norman whispered. "What's that in Tag's mouth?"

James got down on his hands and knees. "I don't believe it!" he gasped. "Hey, Tag— let me have that!"

He reached in Tag's mouth, and triumphantly held up a soggy, crumpled hundred-dollar bill. "It's a little wet with dog spit, but it's okay," he said, as they all cheered quietly.

"Do you suppose that's where the rest of our money went?" Mike asked. "Could *Tag* have taken it all?"

"I don't see how," James said, staring at his sleepy dog. "We didn't let him come out there where the pets were. But maybe—" He looked into Tag's puzzled brown eyes. "Did you take our money, Tag? Where did you put it?"

"That won't do any good," T.J. said crossly. "Dogs can't talk. If he really did take our money, we'll never find it."

"Yeah," Mike agreed. "He can't tell us, any more than this dumb ol' bear could." He gave the bear's head a little kick—and they all froze.

"What was that?" Norman asked. "It sounded like—"

"Like coins jingling!" Pete cried.

Then they were all on their hands and knees, watching as James pried the bear's big jaws open.

"What you doin'?" Ethan asked, opening his eyes and yawning.

But no one answered. They were all cheering, as James pulled handful after handful of money out of the bear's mouth.

"It's all here!" James said, making a quick count. "We can get our jackets after all."

"But how did it *get* there?" Pete asked.

Just then Ethan began to yell. "*My* pennies! Mine! Mine! Mine!"

Norman grabbed the little boy just in time to save James from a kick in the knee.

"Calm down, Ethan," he said. "That's our money. Didn't you know that?"

"Mine!" Ethan insisted. "I found the pennies. I count pennies, see? One, two, three . . ."

"But this isn't just pennies, Ethan!" James explained, holding up a twenty-dollar bill. "And finding it doesn't make it yours." James watched helplessly as Ethan began to sob.

"But Teacher says 'practice!'" Ethan cried. "I need to practice counting!"

"Oh, brother," T.J. muttered. "Little kids. Who needs this?"

"Yeah," Pete agreed. "Someone needs to have a good long talk with your cousin, James."

"Oh, take it easy, guys," Norman said. "After all, he's awfully little. Maybe he didn't know what he was doing."

"Maybe he really thinks pennies are just something to count." James stared unhappily at his little cousin, who was still crying. "Hey, I have an idea. Listen . . ." He whispered something, and his friends nodded. "Hey, Ethan," James said at last, "you and I

74

need to have a little talk, but after that, how would you like a surprise?"

Ethan stopped crying. "A surprise?"

"You'll see," James said. "We'll have our talk while I help you wash your face and brush your hair. Guys, you go tell my mom we've found the money. She probably has the whole house torn apart by now."

Minutes later, they thundered off. All of them were grinning—and their money was safely in James's pocket.

CHAPTER NINE

Red Satin Jackets

"We're going to be the coolest kids in school when we wear these." T.J. beamed, holding a shiny red jacket to her cheek.

"Yeah," Pete agreed. "You were right, T.J. Red *is* the best color."

Ethan hugged his new jacket proudly. "Mine! Thank you."

"You're welcome," Norman said. "In a way, you helped. At least our money isn't in Mean Mitchell's stomach, and you did save Amazon's life."

"But it wasn't right of you to take our

money," Pete reminded the little boy. "You know that now, don't you, Ethan?" Ethan nodded, and Pete ruffled his hair. "Oh well, I'm so happy to finally have these jackets, I've already forgotten about the whole thing."

"Yeah, Pete," T.J. sighed, "but I've been thinking about the way I accused Mean Mitchell. I could have gotten him into a lot of trouble, and this was one time he didn't deserve it. I guess I owe him an apology."

"We all do," James agreed. "We shouldn't have yelled at him in front of Mr. Patelli. Let's hunt him up first thing in the morning and tell him how sorry we are."

Ethan hung his head. "I'm sorry, too," he said. "I just like to count the pennies."

"I can see we're going to have to teach you the difference between pennies and dimes and nickels," James said.

"Not to mention five- and ten- and twenty-dollar bills!" T.J. added.

"Maybe we can do that tomorrow, too. I'd still like to know how you managed to take

77

all that money without us knowing. Right now, I'm having enough trouble believing we were all outwitted by a three-year-old."

The kids arrived at the alterations department and placed their jackets on the counter.

"We'd like to have our names sewn on these jackets," James explained to the woman at the counter. "Will it take long?"

She smiled. "We're not very busy right now. If you'll write your names on these pieces of paper, we can probably have them done by closing time."

Carefully printing their names, the kids pinned the pieces of paper to their jackets.

"And what do you want on *his* jacket?" the woman asked, pointing to Ethan.

"Just his name, I guess," James said. "Ethan."

"No, wait!" Norman exclaimed. "I have a better idea."

He whispered to his friends, who began to laugh.

"That's a great idea," T.J. giggled.

Then they drifted off to the toy and sports departments to browse while they waited.

An hour later, Mike looked at his watch. "Hey," he said, "shouldn't we check on our jackets? They might be ready by now."

They raced down the big staircase, through housewares, past electronics and linens. And there was the alterations lady, about to put a pile of red satin jackets on the counter.

"They're all done," she called. "I think they look great."

Breathlessly, the kids scrambled through the pile until each one had located the right jacket. Quickly, they stuck their arms through the sleeves, zipped the zippers, and spun around to look at themselves in the big mirror on the wall.

"Wow," T.J. breathed, "do we look great, or what?"

"They're even better than I remembered," Pete said.

"And just look at Ethan!" Mike laughed. "That was a great idea, Norman."

James's little cousin was twisting his neck over his shoulder, trying to see the back of his jacket. "What's it say, guys?" he demanded.

Norman grinned. "It says *Critter* because you're the orneriest critter of all," he explained, and Ethan began to pout. "But you're also the smartest critter we've ever had to sit for."

Now Ethan's eyes got big. *"Really?"* he said.

"Really," T.J. promised. "Now let's go show your aunt how sharp you look in your new jacket."

Tag, who had been waiting patiently by the door of the department store, leaped to his feet to greet them as they came out. He sniffed the new jackets and wagged his tail timidly. "I think he's impressed," said James.

The gang walked along quietly, feeling proud in their shiny red satin jackets. They were just getting ready to take a shortcut through the park when a long black car drew up to the curb beside them.

"Children," a familiar voice called, "please come here, darlings, I want to ask you something."

"It's Mrs. Adamson-Smythe," James murmured. "What could *she* want?"

The kids exchanged puzzled looks as they walked over to her car.

"I have a favor to ask," Mrs. Adamson-Smythe explained, as they clustered around the open car window. "You see, I have to leave town again next week, and I was wondering—"

But the kids were already beginning to back away, shaking their heads.

"Uh, sorry, Mrs. Adamson-Smythe," James said, "but it won't be long before school starts again, and we haven't even been swimming once. So in a day or two, just as soon as the last pet's out of my garage, Critter Sitters, Incorporated, is going out of business."

Mrs. Adamson-Smythe looked disappointed. "Oh, I *am* sorry," she said. "And Amazon liked you so much, too! Oh, well,

81

I'm sure you children do deserve *some* vacation. I'll just take Amazon back to my usual place. Good-bye, then—and enjoy the rest of your summer!"

James grinned. "We will," he promised. "Believe me, that's exactly what we're planning to do."

When Mrs. Adamson-Smythe had driven away, the kids collapsed weakly on a nearby park bench. "I can't believe we turned down a chance to listen to opera for a few more weeks!" Norman said. " 'Figaro, Figaro, Figaro!' "

His screechy imitation of Amazon's awful singing made the kids laugh until their sides ached and tears ran down their faces.

"I guess that proves it, though," James said at last, as Tag licked his face and barked happily. "We're the best critter sitters ever."

"We're the best critter sitters in the whole world," T.J. agreed.

"In the whole universe," Norman added.

"Me, too!" said Ethan.

"Hey," Pete suggested, "the swimming pool doesn't close for another couple of hours. Why don't we go check on the animals, then change into our suits and meet there for a swim before dinner?"

"Hooray!" they all cheered. "What a great idea!" As they hurried back to the garage, they could already feel the cool, clear water on their hot faces.